anythink

Bears Make the Best WRITING BUDDIES

written by
CARMEN OLIVER

illustrated by
JEAN CLAUDE

CAPSTONE EDITIONS
a capstone imprint

Bears Make the Best Writing Buddies is published
by Capstone Editions, an imprint of Capstone
1710 Roe Crest Drive
North Mankato, Minnesota 56003
www.capstonepub.com

Library of Congress Cataloging-in-Publication Data
is available on the Library of Congress website.

ISBN: 978-1-68446-081-6 (hardcover)
ISBN: 978-1-68446-082-3 (eBook PDF)

Summary: Adelaide loves writing. Bear loves writing. But Theo
does NOT love writing. Thankfully, Adelaide and Bear are ready
to team up and convince the entire class, including Mrs. Fitz-Pea,
why Bears make the best writing buddies. After all, who better to
teach you how to fish and forage for new ideas than a bear?

Printed and bound in China.
002493

For Bethany, who always gives a friend a hand and
is the best writing buddy a girl could ask for.—C.O.

To João and Luís, all my love.—J.C.

During writing time, Adelaide noticed Theo
staring at his blank paper. He tapped his pencil.
He fanned the pages. Then he pushed his
notebook away with a giant sigh.

Adelaide wrote him a note and passed it along.

Relaxing in a quiet corner, Adelaide found Bear lost in a story.

"Come on," she coaxed. "There's someone who needs our help."

"Adelaide, what are you up to?" Mrs. Fitz-Pea asked.

"Giving a friend a hand," said Adelaide. "Bears make the best writing buddies, and I'm going to tell Theo why."

"They know you never run away from a blank page. They encourage you to stay in your chair, and write the story only you can tell."

"If your ideas burrow and hibernate, Bear takes you fishing and foraging for new ones.

Before you know it, your beehive is buzzing and bursting with topics."

"Next, he reminds you to leave finger spaces as you drop word after word onto the page."

Bears love honey.

"Bears know that even the best writing buddies get frustrated at times, so stand up and stretch and ask, 'What happens next?'"

"And when you do, Bear delivers
a high-five and ROARRRS!"

"He asks you to share details you can see and smell. He asks for details you can hear, taste, or touch."

"There's nothing you can't say when it comes from your heart. Because your voice is *your* voice—no two are the same."

"Whether your story is set in a village or a hot-air balloon, don't leave your main character hanging with nothing to do."

"The sky's the limit, the possibilities are endless.

Keep stacking the action! Reeeeeach for the treetops.

And when your story can't go any further, claw and climb to the perfect ending."

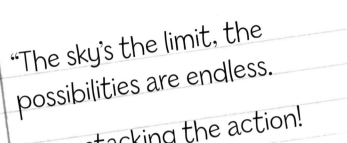

Once there was a hot-air balloon.

"Bears love a good cliffhanger, but they know when it's time to wrap up.

A first draft is just the start of good writing. The real magic begins when you rebuild, reimagine, and rework."

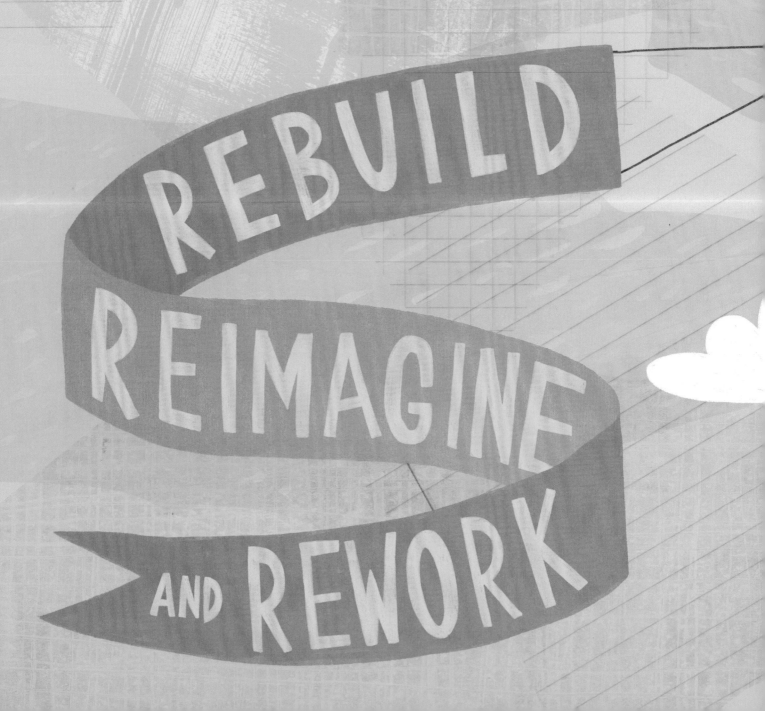

REBUILD

REIMAGINE

AND REWORK

"And that is why bears make the very best writing buddies," Adelaide finished.

Theo snatched his pencil, opened his notebook, and . . .

Bears are very
big, and they like
to eat honey.

. . . wrote page after page and never looked up—along with the rest of the class!

Adelaide wasn't surprised. She picked up her pencil and wrote in her notebook, "To be continued . . ."

Because her story needed a sequel starring . . .

. . . you guessed it—Bear.